The Fish and the Cat

Published by
Princeton Architectural Press
A McEvoy Group company
202 Warren Street
Hudson, New York 12534
Visit our website at www.papress.com

First published in Canada under the title *La mer*
Copyright © 2007 Les Éditions de la Pastèque
Copyright © Marianne Dubuc
Translation rights arranged through the VeroK Agency, Barcelona, Spain.

English edition © 2018 Princeton Architectural Press

ISBN 978-1-61689-505-1

Acquisitions Editor: Rob Shaeffer
Editor: Nina Pick

Special thanks to: Ryan Alcazar, Janet Behning, Nolan Boomer,
Nicola Brower, Abby Bussel, Benjamin English, Jan Cigliano Hartman,
Susan Hershberg, Kristen Hewitt, Lia Hunt, Valerie Kamen,
Jennifer Lippert, Sara McKay, Eliana Miller, Wes Seeley, Sara Stemen,
Marisa Tesoro, Paul Wagner, and Joseph Weston of
Princeton Architectural Press —Kevin C. Lippert, publisher

Library of Congress Cataloging-in-Publication Data
available upon request.

MARIANNE DUBUC

The Fish and the Cat

Princeton Architectural Press · New York

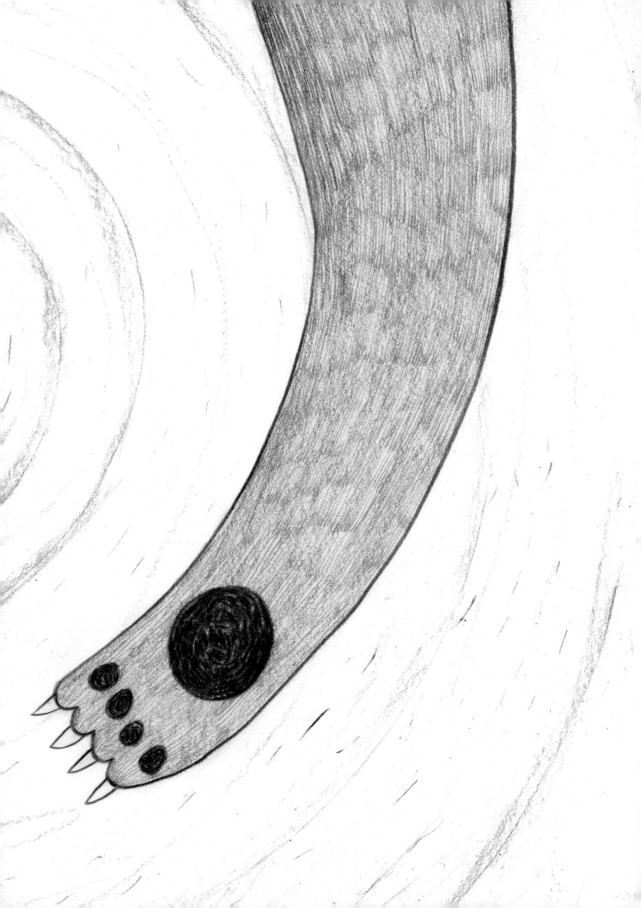

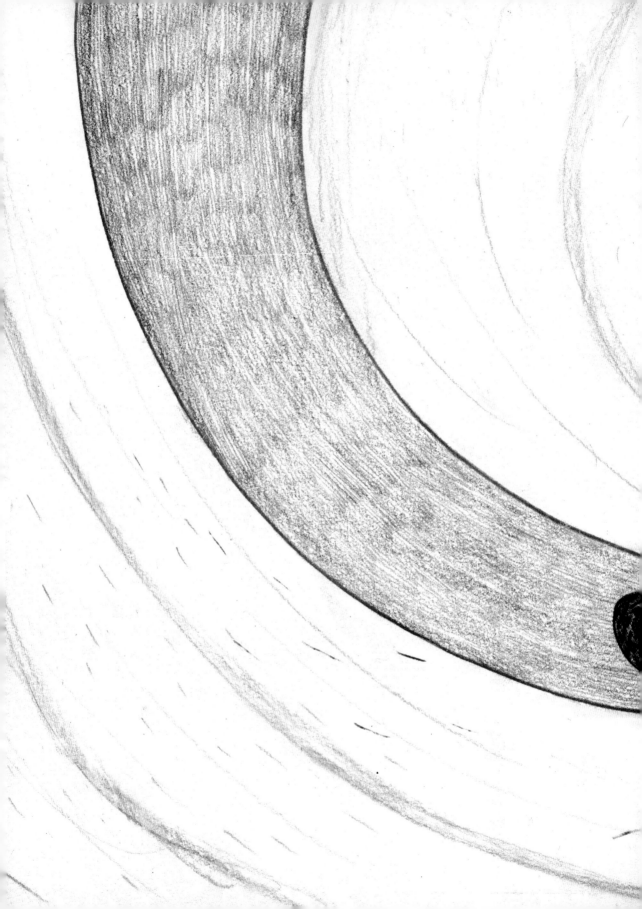

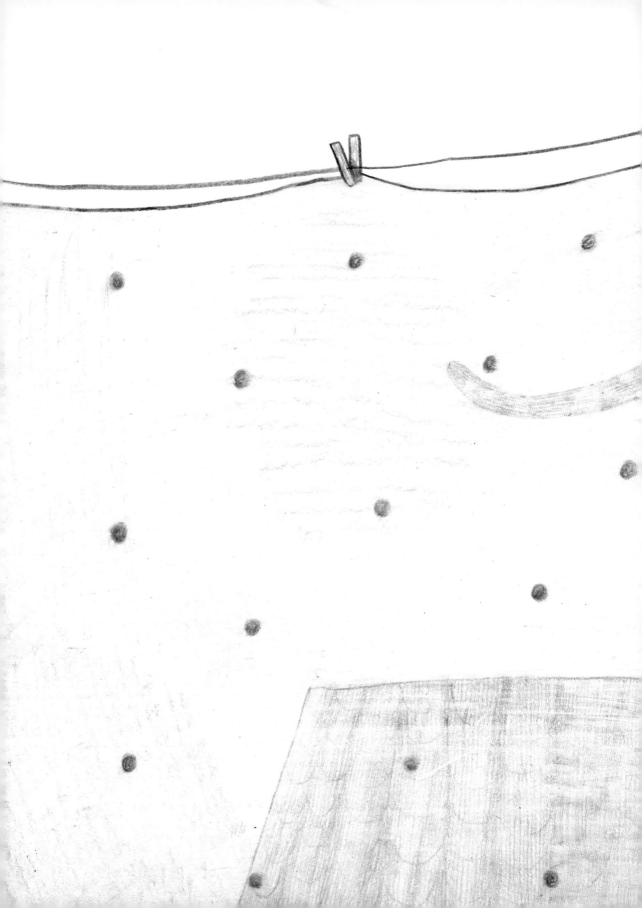

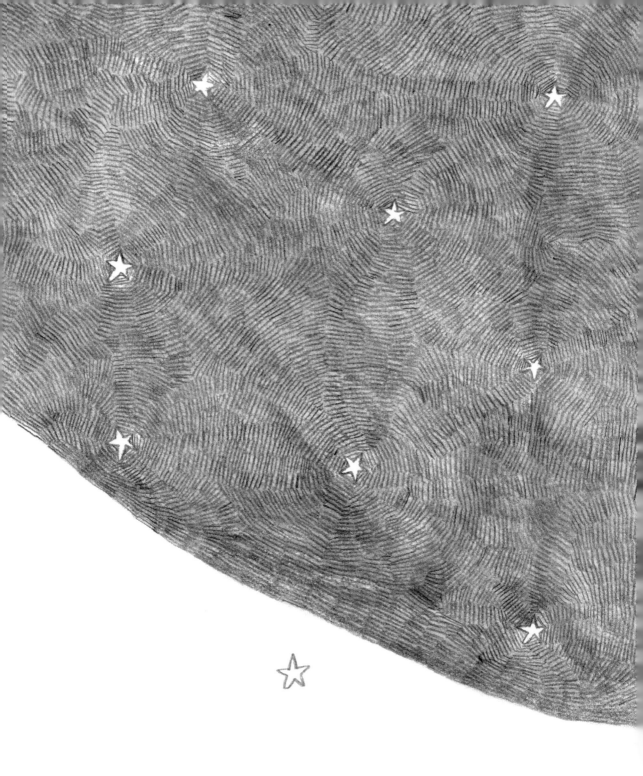

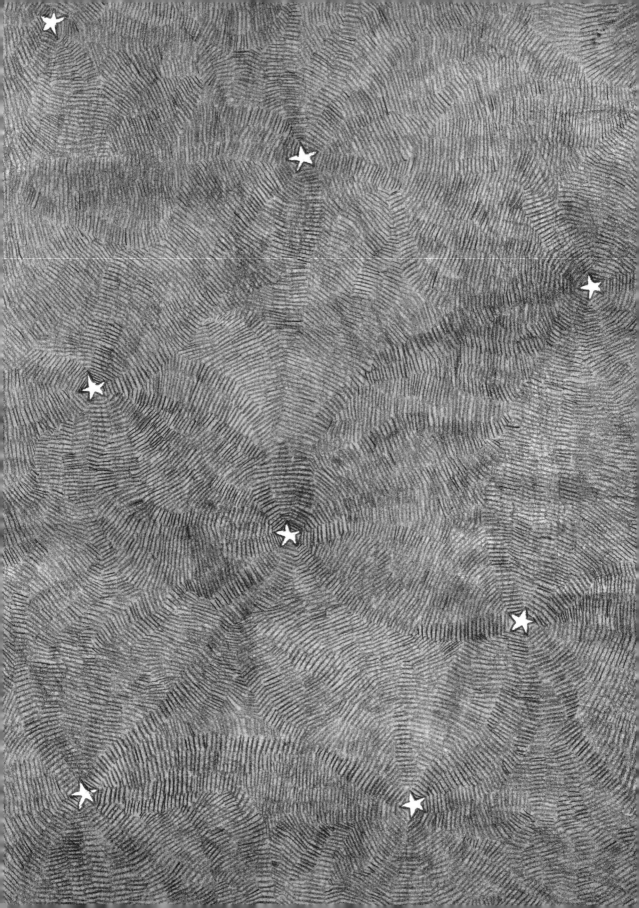

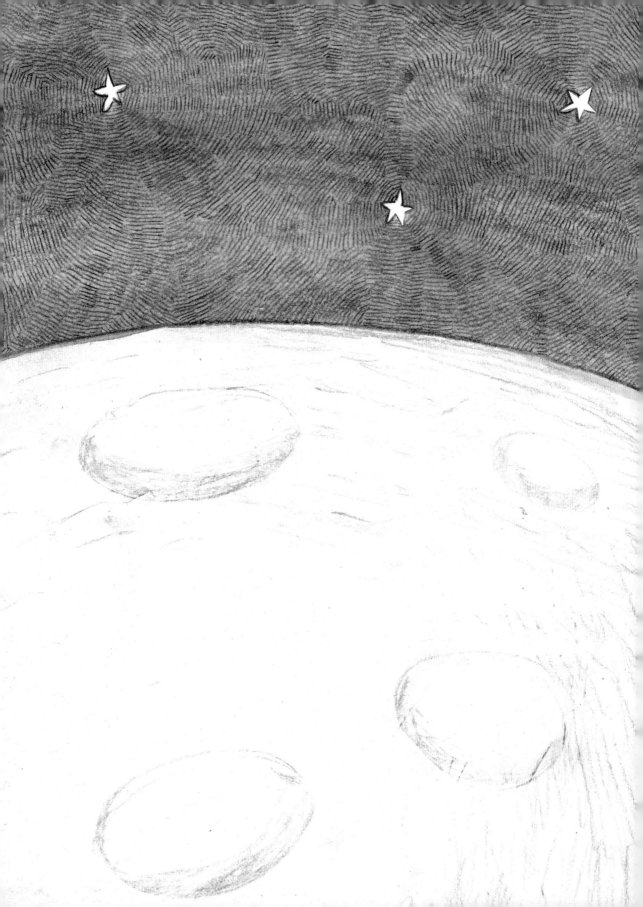

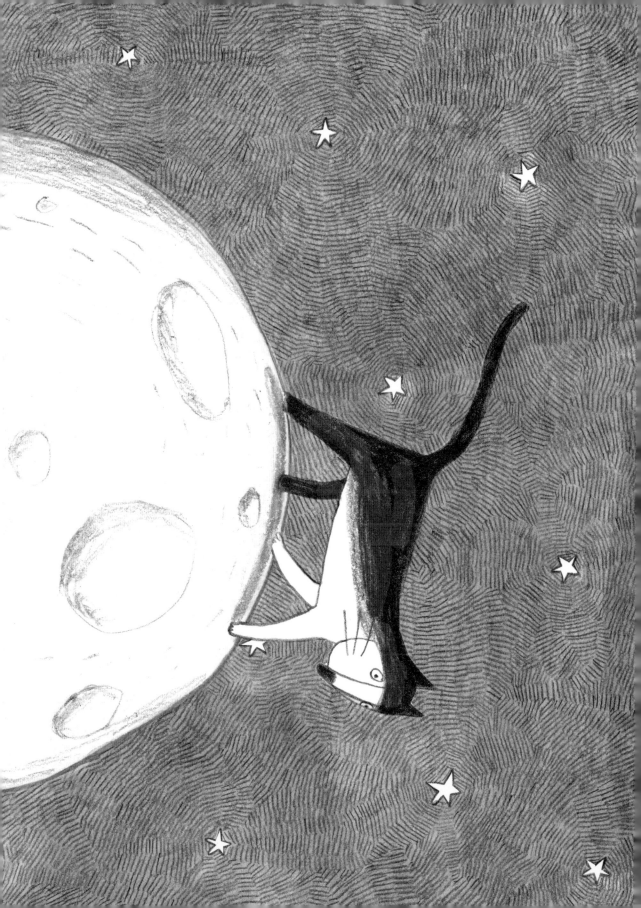